Dear Parents and Educators,

Welcome to Penguin Young Readers! As parents and educators, you know that each child develops at his or her own pace—in terms of speech, critical thinking, and, of course, reading. Penguin Young Readers recognizes this fact. As a result, each Penguin Young Readers book is assigned a traditional easy-to-read level (1–4) as well as a Guided Reading Level (A–P). Both of these systems will help you choose the right book for your child. Please refer to the back of each book for specific leveling information. Penguin Young Readers features esteemed authors and illustrators, stories about favorite characters, fascinating nonfiction, and more!

Angelina Ballerina™
Angelina and the Flower Garden

LEVEL **2**

GUIDED READING LEVEL **I**

This book is perfect for a **Progressing Reader** who:
- can figure out unknown words by using picture and context clues;
- can recognize beginning, middle, and ending sounds;
- can make and confirm predictions about what will happen in the text; and
- can distinguish between fiction and nonfiction.

Here are some **activities** you can do during and after reading this book:
- Setting: The setting of the story is where it takes place. Discuss the setting or settings of this story. Use some evidence from the text to describe the setting.
- Sight Words: Sight words are frequently used words that readers know just by looking at them. These words are not "sounded out" or "decoded"; rather, they are known instantly, on sight. As you are reading the story, have the child point out the sight words listed below.

an	her	of	she	what
has	must	old	then	with

Remember, sharing the love of reading with a child is the best gift you can give!

—Bonnie Bader, EdM
   Penguin Young Readers program

*Penguin Young Readers are leveled by independent reviewers applying the standards developed by Irene Fountas and Gay Su Pinnell in *Matching Books to Readers: Using Leveled Books in Guided Reading*, Heinemann, 1999.

HiT entertainment

PENGUIN YOUNG READERS
An Imprint of Penguin Random House LLC

ISBN 978-0-448-49006-9   10 9 8 7 6 5 4 3 2 1

Angelina and the Flower Garden

by Lana Jacobs

illustrated by Artful Doodlers

inspired by the classic children's book series by author
Katharine Holabird and illustrator Helen Craig

Penguin Young Readers
An Imprint of Penguin Random House

Angelina is happy.

She loves to be with her friends.

The sun is out.

The birds are singing.

Spring is here!

Angelina has an idea.

"Let's plant a flower garden,"

she says.

Angelina digs a hole.

Alice plants a tiny flower

in the hole.

Polly pats the soil on top.

They all pour water

on the ground.

The mouselings twirl and leap

in their new garden.

Grow, flowers, grow!

Miss Lilly is proud

of the mouselings.

She is proud of their hard work.

It is time to go home.

The mouselings are covered

in dirt and mud.

What a fun day!

At home, Angelina tells her family

about the garden.

"I can't wait to go

back to school tomorrow

to see our garden," she says.

The next day, Angelina goes
to see the garden.

Oh no!

What happened to the flowers?

"The flowers have been trampled,"

says Miss Lilly.

"The birds must have been happy

to see the garden, too," she says.

Angelina is sad.

All their hard work is ruined.

Wait!

Angelina has an idea.

"Why don't we make a garden

for the birds *and* the flowers?"

she says.

What a great idea!

The mouselings get right to work.

Angelina and her friends
build a birdhouse.
Alice *pirouettes* as they hang up
the birdhouse.

Then they gather twigs

to build a nest.

Polly fills up the birdbath.

Now the birds will have

lots of places to rest!

Angelina plants a new batch of tiny flowers.

"Now the garden is ready
for spring!" says Angelina.

Suddenly a bird flies

into the garden.

He splashes in the birdbath.

Another bird flies

into the birdhouse.

Angelina's plan worked!

It is time to celebrate

with a new spring dance.

Angelina is so happy

to welcome spring

with her friends.

Her old friends—

and her new friends!